OTTO
GOES NORTH

ULRIKA KESTERE

GECKO PRESS

Far up in the north you'll find a blueberry-blue house with a grass roof. There lives a lynx called Lisa and a little bear called Nils. The red house on the right is the sauna. You can't imagine how hot it gets in there.

One day Lisa was on the roof, mowing the grass. Little Nils was setting out afternoon tea in the garden. They wanted everything to be nice for their friend Otto, a lemur, who was coming to visit. He'd been cycling for several months to get there. Maybe even years. A very long time in any case.

Look, here he comes!

Otto was in very good shape. You have to be if you're going to cycle for hundreds of days.

His bike was red with a large shiny bell. Otto would ring it like mad, enough to be annoying. He rang it as soon as he saw Lisa and Nils.

Pling! Pling! Pling! "Here I am!" he called.

The friends all hugged and said hello.

"It's been ages!" said Otto.

"You've grown so tall!" said Lisa.

"Such beautiful weather!" said Nils.

Otto wanted to tell them all that had happened on his journey.
Among other things, he'd met a hedgehog who'd lost her gloves and
a goat who just wanted to be left alone.

"...and this evening I'll see the northern lights at last!" said Otto.
"I'll paint them so I can hang the picture on my wall at home."

"Good idea—otherwise you might forget what they look like," said Lisa.
"Nils and I keep forgetting. We're surprised every time."

At sunset Otto padded off to the nearest cliff with his paints and brushes. The air was so cold that his nose turned icy. Otto set up his easel and made the first brushstrokes. But before long he began to freeze. Really freeze. He shook so hard he couldn't hold the brush steady. Every stroke became a zigzag.

"Shi-vv-vv-vers!" said Otto through shaking teeth.

When Otto came back his nose was red and runny. He held his painting up sadly to show Nils and Lisa.

"S-s-so c-cold…" he sniffed, "it g-got s-soo sh-shaky and ug-ugly."

"But how come you're so cold when you have fur like us?" asked Nils.

"It's hot where I come from," said Otto. "My fur isn't like yours."

"Gosh," said Nils. "I didn't know there was a difference between fur and fur."

Nils and Lisa took Otto off to the sauna with
a cup of hot blueberry soup.

"You'd better sleep here tonight," said Lisa.
"Then you'll keep warm."

They were worried about Otto. He needed something warm
to wear. Could they make him something? By sticking some
moss together, maybe? That's what Nils thought.

Nils and Lisa didn't have many books. Two, to be precise. One was a detective novel about a moose who found the forest a little too mysterious. It was good. They'd read it hundreds of times. The other book was about wool. It was a present from Lena the fox. Lisa sat with it in the armchair by the fire. Maybe it could teach them how to knit.

"What does the book say?" Nils asked the next morning.

"I don't know. Halfway through, I realized I'd forgotten how to read," said Lisa. "But if I understand the pictures correctly, we should start by collecting a sack of soft wool. From a sheep. But I don't know any sheep. Do you?"

"Not very well. But can't we use our own wool?" asked Nils. "I'm soft. Even cuddly."

"I'm soft too. Probably much softer than a sheep," said Lisa.

The friends began to comb their fur. It wasn't
a competition, but you could say that Lisa won,
because she combed out such a lot.

Nils was a bit cross. "Why do you have so much fur?"

"Well," said Lisa, "maybe you have less because you're smaller."

"Who are you calling small?"

"Come on, don't be grumpy, Nils." Lisa giggled as she collected
all the tufts of fur into a sack.

In the book about wool there was a picture of the steering wheel thing they needed to turn the fur into yarn. Nils and Lisa didn't have one, but their friend Lena did. So they took the fur to her house and she showed them how it worked.

Nils wondered if Lena would spin the fur for them since she already knew how to do it. But she wouldn't. "It's fun learning new things, Nils," she said. "And it makes you smarter, too."

So Nils spun while Lisa carded the fur.

They gave Lena a basket of cinnamon buns to say thank you, then they rolled their ball of wool towards home.

Nils was proud. "Just think: we did it all ourselves!" he said. "I'm pretty clever!"

There was silence for a moment.

Then Lisa practically shouted, "Well, I'm pretty clever too!"

"Stop yelling," said Nils. "It's not a competition."

When they got home they checked on Otto in the sauna.
His nose was still red.

"How are you, Otto?" asked Nils.

"Not so good," Otto sniffed. "I'm sick. I think I'll stay in the
sauna today. It's so nice and warm in here."

"We have a surprise for you, Otto, for when you're better,"
said Lisa.

"That's nice," said Otto. "I hope it's more blueberry soup."

It was time to dye the wool. In the pantry they found the leftovers from dinner. Some onions and red cabbage. They put some wool aside and divided the rest between three pots of water. The red onion went in one, the yellow onion in another, and the red cabbage in the third. What do you think happened?

When the yarn was ready, they had new shades of yellow, red and blue. Lisa hung it up to dry in the garden while Nils took hot blueberry soup out to Otto.

Once the wind had dried the yarn, Nils began to knit.
Lisa's paws were too clumsy to hold the needles.

"It's a bit annoying that I have to do all the knitting,
just because your paws are too thick," Nils complained.
"This is taking ages."

When they were almost finished, Otto began to feel well again.
He left the sauna, and at last Nils and Lisa gave him his surprise.
Otto was very moved. He'd never been given anything so fine before.

"I knitted it!" said Nils.

"Do you like it?" asked Lisa.

Otto was so snug he felt almost as if he was home
in the south. He stood outside painting for several
hours without feeling the slightest bit cold.

He gave Nils and Lisa the painting as a present, because he would
take the northern lights they'd made him home as a memory. Then for many
days the friends played games, inside in the warmth and outside in the cold.

At last it was time for Otto to bike home to the warm south,
and he said goodbye for now.

Back home, Otto hung his northern lights on the wall, among all his other artworks. They help him remember his friends and the beautiful landscape of the north. They can stay there until next time he visits Nils and Lisa!

This edition first published in 2019 by Gecko Press
PO Box 9335, Wellington 6141, New Zealand
info@geckopress.com

English-language edition © Gecko Press Ltd 2019

Original title: Ottos Ulliga Tröja
© Text and illustrations: Ulrika Kestere 2018
© Bokförlaget Opal AB 2018

The illustrations are created with graphite pencil
and acrylic paint on paper then reworked digitally.

Translated by Julia Marshall
Edited by Penelope Todd
Typesetting by Vida Kelly
Printed in China by Everbest Printing Co. Ltd,
an accredited ISO 14001 & FSC-certified printer

ISBN hardback: 978-1-776572-41-0
ISBN paperback: 978-1-776572-42-7

For more curiously good books, visit geckopress.com